LUCY AND THE PIRATES

For Mary, Paul, Anneke, Jasmin and Bunny by MH

First published simultaneously in
Great Britain and Canada in 1996 by
Tradewind Books Limited
29 Lancaster Park, Richmond, Surrey TW10 6AB England,
& Tradewind Books Limited
2216 Stephens Street, Vancouver, British Columbia V6K 3W6, Canada.

Typography by Philippa Bramson

Originated in Italy by Typongraph, Verona

Printed in Singapore by Imago Publishing Limited

Cataloguing-in-Publication Data for this book is
available from the British Library

Canadian Cataloguing in Publication Data

Petrie, Glen.
Lucy and the pirates

ISBN 1-896580-02-5

I. Harrison, Matilda, 1962- II. Title
PZ7.P47Lu 199   j823'.914   C95-910713-4

LUCY AND THE PIRATES

Glen Petrie

Illustrated by Matilda Harrison

LONDON/VANCOUVER

ucy lived with her mother who kept a shop on the quayside at Southsea. Two years before, Lucy's father took berth as sea-cook on a big merchant ship, the *Prospect of Deal*. It set sail for the West Indies but disappeared without trace.

Lucy hoped that her father was still alive. 'Perhaps he has been captured by pirates,' she thought to herself.

One day Parson Smirke came into the shop, as he often did, to comfort Lucy's mother. 'Now that your father is gone you must do more to help your mother,' he said.

'I do help Mama, sir,' Lucy replied. 'I help you in the shop, don't I Mama?'

'Oh yes. Lucy helps me ever so much,' said Lucy's mother.

'It's your duty to go out and earn your living, Lucy,' said Parson Smirke. 'My cousins, the Misses Weevil, need a maid to scrub the floors and do their washing and ironing.'

Lucy didn't want to work for the Misses Weevil; they scowled at her in church on Sundays, even when she was behaving properly.

That night, Lucy and her mother were woken by a loud knocking. They tiptoed downstairs. There, standing on the doorstep, was the strangest-looking man they had ever seen. He had one glass eye, one ear missing, one empty sleeve and a wooden leg. He held a heavy leather purse in his hand.

'Don't be afeared o' Half-a-Man, my dearies – they calls me Half-a-Man, d'ye see, 'cause I been in the King's wars and there's naught but half o' me left! Half-a-Man has sailed across the world to find a Miss Lucy Masters. A certain shipmate of Half-a-Man says: "Give Miss Lucy Masters this purse from me. Tell her to spend it all on the book-learning and the fine clothes and such, as befits a lady of quality."'

Lucy and her mother took the purse.

'Forty pieces of Spanish gold. That's what's in it,' said the strange-looking man. 'And Half-a-Man, he ain't laid a finger on one of 'em, may the Devil take his soul if he tell a lie!'

'Papa must have sent it!' cried Lucy. 'Papa is alive!'

The strange-looking man vanished. Outside there was nothing but moonlight and a chill wind blowing across the empty quay.

One afternoon, Horace Maltby, captain of the *Hornbeam*, came into the shop with several of his crew and a passenger, Lady Marietta Tarrant, whom Lucy thought the most elegant lady she had ever seen. They were bound for the West Indies but, before they set sail, they wanted to buy lamp oil and candles, soap and linseed, a barrel of apples, big woolly sweaters, one cask of lime juice and casks of rum.

Lady Marietta offered to take Lucy to see the *Hornbeam*. As they strolled along the quay, Lucy told Lady Marietta about her father. 'I wish I could sail to the West Indies to find him.'said Lucy. 'even if it is thousands of miles away and there are pirates and cannibals and things!'

Lady Marietta said, 'Lucy, I'm sailing on the *Hornbeam* to the West Indies. My husband, General Sir Frederick Tarrant, is the officer commanding the soldiers in Spanish Town. My maid doesn't want to come with me – she's afraid of being captured by pirates and being made to walk the plank. You're not the sort of girl who is afraid of pirates, are you?'

'I don't think so,' replied Lucy.

'Would you like to be my maid and sail to the West Indies with me?'

'Oh yes, please!' cried Lucy.

Lady Marietta asked her mother if she might take Lucy with her. To Lucy's surprise, she heard her mother say yes.

On a bright fresh morning the *Hornbeam* put out of Southsea. The sailors climbed the rigging and unfurled their sails which billowed in the wind.

Lucy stood on deck waving goodbye to her mother. Parson Smirke, who was with Lucy's mother, smiled broadly and waved his handkerchief. The Misses Weevil stood there scowling, just as they always did in church on Sundays. Lucy was sorry to leave her mother, but not at all sorry to leave Parson Smirke and the Misses Weevil.

On the voyage there wasn't a lot of room for Lucy to run around and, in any case, everybody was too busy sailing the ship to play. But, she soon made friends with Wilkins, Captain Maltby's cabin boy.

'Lady Marietta is taking me to the West Indies to find my father, Lucy said. 'He was sea-cook on the *Prospect of Deal*, when it disappeared.'

'Captured by Pirates, I daresay!' Wilkins suggested cheerfully.

Wilkins told her stories about his past. He had been born a slave on a sugar plantation on the island of Antigua, and one dark night he escaped and ran away to sea.

'Life on the *Hornbeam* can be hard,' he told Lucy. 'But,' he went on, 'everybody on board treats me as a free man.'

Lucy thought of having to scrub the floors and do all the washing and ironing for the Misses Weevil for no pay at all.

'I don't think *anybody* should be anybody else's slave,' Lucy told Wilkins.

One day Wilkins said to Lucy, 'I'm going up to the crow's nest to be the lookout. Would you like to come too?' She tilted her head to look up at the mast. The crow's nest seemed very high.

'I think my dress would get in the way,' she told Wilkins. But Wilkins said, 'I've got a spare set of sea-clothes. You can borrow them.'

'Yes please,' Lucy replied bravely, and when she had changed into boy's clothes, she climbed high up the rigging with Wilkins.

'Don't look down,' he told her. 'Not until you get used to it.'

Lady Marietta spotted Lucy up in the sky above the sails. 'Oh Lucy!' she shrieked. 'Do take care!'

Lucy reached the top at last. The sailors shouted, 'Hurray for Lucy! She's a real sailor, and no mistake!'

Lucy looked through Wilkins' telescope. 'Look sharp,' he teased her, 'and who knows you might spy a ship with your father on board!'

Suddenly she saw a ship. It didn't look like the *Prospect of Deal*! 'There's a ship!' she called to Wilkins. 'But its mast has broken. Men are lying all over the deck. Oh! and there are stains everywhere. It's blood – I'm sure it's blood! They must be ever so badly hurt!'

Wilkins took the telescope. He shouted down to the Captain, 'HMS *Torbay*, sir! On the port bow! She's been in a fight, sir! The mainmast's shot away, and she's holed above the water-line!'

The sailors rowed Captain Maltby out on to HMS *Torbay*. Lucy and Wilkins went with him. Captain Hancock RN, the Master of HMS *Torbay* , told them what had happened – that he and his men had spotted a notorious pirate, the wicked Captain Blacktooth, in his forty-gun ship the *Blacktooth's Revenge*. They had pursued it and given battle.

He said, 'Just as we were about to capture the *Blacktooth's Revenge*, two more pirate ships appeared! They were commanded by Blacktooth's wives, Susan Redshanks and Gunpowder Jane. Those two must be the rudest, roughest females a man ever set eyes on! We beat off Blacktooth's ships, but it was a deuced close-run thing!'

Before returning to the *Hornbeam* with Wilkins and Captain Maltby, Lucy helped wash and bandage the wounded sailors on deck. 'God bless us,' they told her, 'if you ain't the prettiest, kindest young female in the whole world!'

And so the *Hornbeam* continued with a fair wind for Spanish Town, Jamaica. Lucy often sat up in the rigging with Wilkins. She could not help thinking it would be wonderful to be a pirate – and to capture a ship with Parson Smirke on board, and the Misses Weevil! She would make Parson Smirke walk the plank and make the Misses Weevil scrub the decks.

One afternoon, her daydream was suddenly interrupted as Wilkins pointed out over the stern and shouted down to Captain Maltby, '*Pirates Ho!*'

The *Hornbeam* was pursued by the three pirate ships. There was a ferocious battle and Captain Blacktooth and his two wives, Susan Redshanks and Gunpowder Jane, boarded the *Hornbeam*. Captain Maltby was disarmed and tied up.

'Aha!' cried Captain Blacktooth when he saw Lady Marietta, 'I been thinking as how I might take another wife – seeing as how my other two aren't as pretty as they was!' He spotted Lucy standing beside Lady Marietta.

'Stab me vitals!' he cried. 'And who might this toothsome little morsel be, eh, my hearties?'

'This is my shipmate, Luke,' said Wilkins.

'And who might you be?' roared Captain Blacktooth.

'I'm Wilkins, if it please you, sir,' Wilkins replied. 'What ran away to sea 'cause I didn't want to be a slave no more. And this here, my shipmate Luke, he were arrested for stealing a handkerchief. They were going to hang him, sir, only he ran away like me, sir,' said Wilkins.

'Are you two scraps ready to swear loyalty to the sacred flag of the King of Death and join us as pirates?'

'Aye aye, sir!' Wilkins said quickly.

Lady Marietta, Lucy and Wilkins were rowed across to the *Blacktooth's Revenge* while the pirates looted the *Hornbeam's* cargo and Susan Redshanks and Gunpowder Jane fought over Lady Marietta's jewellery chest.

Lady Marietta said disapprovingly to Lucy and Wilkins, 'I do hope neither of you *really* is going to be a pirate!'

'I don't think so,' Lucy said. She was rather shocked by the behaviour of Blacktooth's wives.

The pirates marooned Captain Maltby and his crew on a small island nearby. They might, if they were lucky, be picked up by a passing ship, or they might die of thirst and starvation. After removing all the cargo from the *Hornbeam*, the pirates blew her up. She sank slowly until all that could be seen of her was the topmast above the waves.

Lucy, Wilkins and Lady Marietta were climbing aboard the *Blacktooth's Revenge* when Wilkins whispered to Lucy, 'That man standing over there in the hatchway is staring at you as though he recognizes you.' Lucy looked up and gasped. The man was wearing a chef's white hat. She could hardly keep the excitement to herself.

She whispered to Wilkins, 'It's my papa!'

That night, the pirates held a party and watched Captain Blacktooth dance a hornpipe with Susan Redshanks and Gunpowder Jane. All the pirates knew that if they didn't shout 'Hurrah' and 'Encore!' or 'Gosh! How wonderful!' they would be thrown overboard to feed the sharks. So they all shouted and fired off the cannon and made a terrible noise.

When at last they had shouted themselves hoarse and drunk all the rum, the pirates fell asleep and snored loudly. Lucy and Wilkins sat with Lady Marietta in the moonlight. They spotted one of the pirates tiptoeing towards them.

'Papa!' Lucy exclaimed. She gave him a big hug. 'I knew you were still alive even before Half-a-Man gave the Spanish gold to Mama and me! And now I've found you.'

Lucy's father told them how his ship was captured by Captain Blacktooth and renamed *Blacktooth's Revenge*. All the crew were made to walk the plank except him. He was saved because the pirates didn't have a proper sea-cook and they hadn't had a hot dinner for as long as they could remember.

The pirate ships had been at sea for many months and were running out of food and water. Captain Blacktooth set course for a tropical island where the pirates unloaded the cargoes and then pulled the ships onto the dry sand of the beach.

'Nothing is going to attack us through the jungle,' laughed Captain Blacktooth. 'Because there ain't a mortal soul what knows we're here! We'll mount the cannon on the rocks facing out to sea.'

Captain Blacktooth tied Lady Marietta to a tree. Lucy and Wilkins, with the younger pirates, were made to scrape the seaweed and barnacles off the ships' bottoms. Their arms began to ache terribly.

'It's as bad as doing housework for the Misses Weevil!' sighed Lucy.

'It ain't worse than being a slave!' Wilkins told her.

Later that afternoon, Captain Blacktooth told Wilkins and Lucy to fetch some ice-cold water from a waterfall up among the rocky peaks high above the jungle.

'Take a bucket each. Mind ye don't spill none, neither, or I'll have ye thrown into the sea for the sharks – and the Devil can take what's left of ye!'

Lucy and Wilkins climbed upwards through the jungle. It was dark and gloomy under the leaves. A large snake slithered through the branches. A black cat-like creature crossed the path and disappeared into the undergrowth. They were greatly relieved when they emerged from the jungle and could see the waterfall hanging against the cliff above.

They got soaking wet filling their buckets and sat together in the baking sun to get dry. Far below, over the tops of the trees, they saw the pirate ships lying on their sides on the sand of the bay.

Lucy looked down at the other side of the island. She couldn't believe her eyes. There was another ship at anchor and men camped on the beach. She spotted the White Ensign – the flag of the Royal Navy – flying over the camp. She tugged at Wilkins' sleeve and pointed.

'Look, Wilkins! It's HMS *Torbay* ! They've mended the mast! Come on, let's go down and tell Captain Hancock where the pirates are. Now we can rescue Lady Marietta and my papa!

She grabbed Wilkins by the arm and pulled him after her.

They were out of breath when they reached the shore where the crew of HMS *Torbay* were encamped. A sailor took them to Captain Hancock's tent.

'Why!' the Captain cried out. 'Deuce take me if it ain't the cabin boy and the little maid from the *Hornbeam*!'

Wilkins and Lucy told him what had happened to them. They explained how Captain Maltby and his crew were marooned and left to die of hunger and thirst.

'Captain Blacktooth means to marry Lady Marietta as his third wife,' Lucy told him. 'He's keeping her tied to a tree.'

'Is he, by Heaven! We must go and rescue her!' exclaimed Hancock. 'We'll attack the pirate camp tonight!'

Under cover of darkness, Wilkins led the marines silently along the shore to capture the pirates' cannon. At the same time, Lucy crept up to the beached ships looking for Lady Marietta. She found her and cut her loose. She and Lady Marietta hid under some trees. Wilkins and the Marines fired the cannon to signal the attack. Captain Hancock and his men charged with bugles blowing and drums beating.

Captain Blacktooth and his men, taken by surprise, were all captured. Well – nearly all – Susan Redshanks and Gunpowder Jane managed to escape into the jungle.

Captain Hancock and his men refloated the *Blacktooth's Revenge*. They repainted its real name on its stern – *Prospect of Deal*. They put back its cargo and remounted its cannon. Captain Blacktooth and his wicked crew were chained up in the bilges of HMS *Torbay* . Then both ships sailed to the island where Captain Maltby and the crew of the *Hornbeam* had been marooned.

Captain Maltby and his men were desperately hungry and thirsty when they came aboard the *Prospect of Deal*. Lucy's father made a large pot of tea for them and cooked their favourite meal.

Captain Hancock handed over the *Prospect of Deal* to captain Maltby and the crew of the *Hornbeam*. Captain Maltby tried to say 'thank you' but Captain Hancock wouldn't hear of it.

Against a cloudless sky, HMS *Torbay* escorted the *Prospect of Deal* into Spanish Town harbour. There was a military band waiting to welcome them; the King's Governor was there, wearing his magnificent plumed hat, with Lady Marietta's husband, General Sir Frederick Tarrant, looking splendid in his scarlet uniform. When they had disembarked, Lady Marietta told the king's Governor about Lucy's and Wilkins' extraordinary bravery.

Lucy and Wilkins were taken in the Governor's carriage to his mansion. All the way the church bells rang out; there were people lining the pavements, waving and throwing flowers into the carriage. Captain Blacktooth and his pirates were immediately locked up in prison.

That night there was a great firework display and dancing in the streets. There was a great banquet at the Governor's mansion. Later, they all went out into the courtyard. In the light from the fireworks, Lucy and Wilkins, Lady Marietta and her husband the General, and Lucy's father and the King's Governor's wife danced a fandango.

The King's governor didn't dance a fandango because,

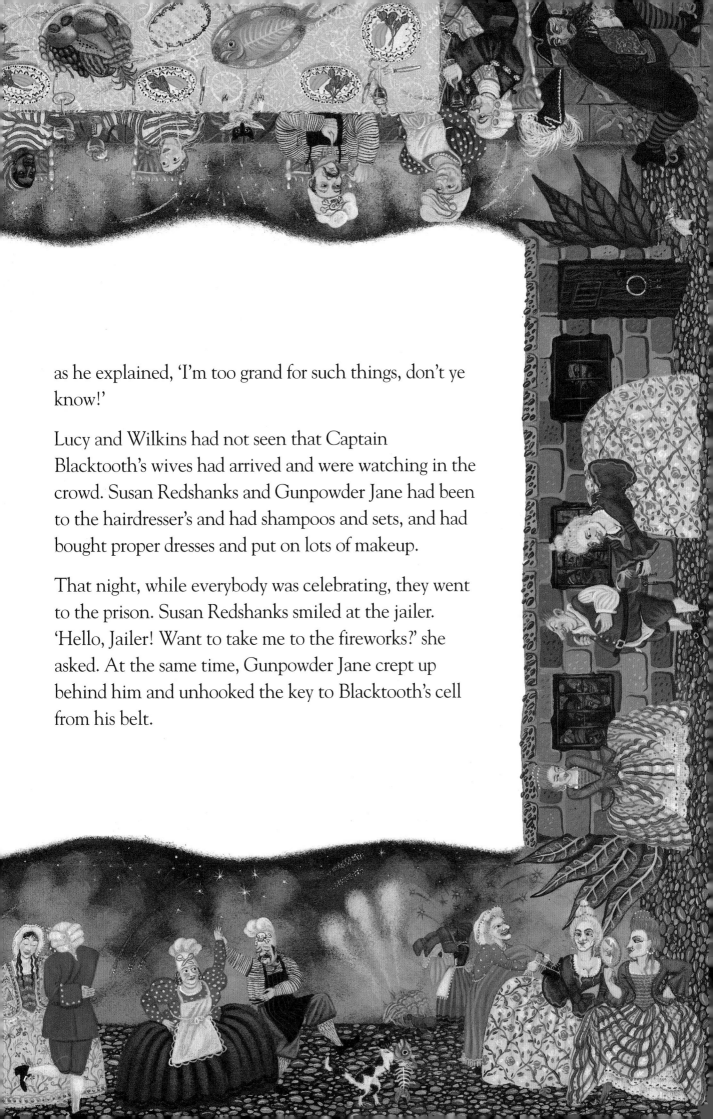

as he explained, 'I'm too grand for such things, don't ye know!'

Lucy and Wilkins had not seen that Captain Blacktooth's wives had arrived and were watching in the crowd. Susan Redshanks and Gunpowder Jane had been to the hairdresser's and had shampoos and sets, and had bought proper dresses and put on lots of makeup.

That night, while everybody was celebrating, they went to the prison. Susan Redshanks smiled at the jailer. 'Hello, Jailer! Want to take me to the fireworks?' she asked. At the same time, Gunpowder Jane crept up behind him and unhooked the key to Blacktooth's cell from his belt.

Lucy and Wilkins were given a rich reward for their part in the capture of Captain Blacktooth and his men. Before boarding the *Prospect of Deal* for the voyage home, Lucy asked Wilkins if he would come home with her to England.

'I'm going to sail round the world, 'till I find a country where there aren't any slaves' he told her. 'I'll buy a house there. Then, maybe I'll become master of my own ship, and sail to Southsea.'

'Oh please!' pleaded Lucy. 'And then we'll sail away together and have more adventures!'

When at last they had crossed the ocean, Lucy brought her father home. 'Look Mama!' she cried. 'Look who I've brought!' Her mother came running out into the street and gave huge hugs to both Lucy and her Papa.

But Parson Smirke was not smiling. He was just about to ask Lucy's mother to marry him and live at the Misses Weevil's house.

With Lucy's reward money and the Spanish gold her father had sent her, there was no need for her father ever to have to go to sea again, or for Lucy to be anybody's maid.